Silvermist
and the
Ladybug
Curse

Silvermist
and the
Ladybug
Curse

WRITTEN BY
GAIL HERMAN

ILLUSTRATED BY
ADRIENNE BROWN, CHARLES PICKENS
& DENISE SHIMABUKURO

HarperCollins *Children's Books*

First published in the USA by Disney Press,
114 Fifth Avenue, New York, New York, 10011-5690.

First published in Great Britain in 2007
by HarperCollins Children's Books.
HarperCollins Children's Books is a division of
HarperCollins Publishers,
77 - 85 Fulham Palace Road, Hammersmith, London, W6 8JB.

The HarperCollins Children's Books website is
www.harpercollinschildrensbooks.co.uk

978-0-00-726291-5
0-00-726291-4

1

Printed and bound in the UK

Visit disneyfairies.com

This book is proudly printed on paper which contains wood
from well managed forests, certified in accordance with
the rules of the Forest Stewardship Council.
For more information about FSC,
please visit www.fsc-uk.org

Mixed Sources
Product group from well-managed
forests and other controlled sources
www.fsc.org Cert no. SW-COC-1806
© 1996 Forest Stewardship Council
FSC

All About Fairies

IF YOU HEAD towards the second star on your right and fly straight on till morning, you'll come to Never Land, a magical island where mermaids play and children never grow up.

When you arrive, you might hear something like the tinkling of little bells. Follow that sound and you'll find Pixie Hollow, the secret heart of Never Land.

A great old maple tree grows in Pixie

Hollow, and in it live hundreds of fairies and sparrow men. Some of them can do water magic, others can fly like the wind, and still others can speak to animals. You see, Pixie Hollow is the Never fairies' kingdom, and each fairy who lives there has a special, extraordinary talent.

Not far from the Home Tree, nestled in the branches of a hawthorn, is Mother Dove, the most magical creature of all. She sits on her egg, watching over the fairies, who in turn watch over her. For as long as Mother Dove's egg stays well and whole, no one in Never Land will ever grow old.

Once, Mother Dove's egg was broken. But we are not telling the story of the egg here. Now it is time for Silvermist's tale...

Silvermist
and the
Ladybug
Curse

1

SUNLIGHT SPARKLED ON the cool, clear waters of Havendish Stream. Silvermist waded in. She took the oak-leaf cover off her tiny birchbark canoe.

She lifted her face and sniffed the air. "Mmmm-mmmm."

Silvermist was a water-talent fairy. She loved everything about water: the sight, the sounds, and the feel of it. And she especially loved the damp, sharp smell of it.

But this day, the smells of freshly baked muffins and cakes were mixed in with the smell of the stream. The fairies and sparrow men of Pixie Hollow were getting ready for a picnic – a special picnic on an island not far from the shore. Water fairies filled birchbark canoes with food, drinks, and supplies. Grass-weaving talents carried picnic blankets. Harvest talents brought fresh berries. Baking talents flew over to the boats with picnic treats.

Silvermist smiled as she stepped back to the shore. "It all smells delicious!" she told Dulcie, a baking talent. "This picnic will be the best ever."

Dulcie nodded. She held out a basket for Silvermist to take. "Here are some muffins and berry juice."

"I'll help!" said Silvermist's friend Fira, a light-talent fairy, as she reached for the basket to put into the canoe.

Silvermist smiled at Fira. Some fairies thought it odd that they were friends. The two were so different. Fira was quick tempered and fiery, while Silvermist was calm and quiet.

They were opposites, but they were drawn to each other.

Rani, another water talent, pushed off in her canoe. She began to paddle towards the island.

One by one, the rest of the water fairies followed. The Fairy Ferry was under way. Other talents hovered above the canoes. They trailed the boats towards the island.

"Come on, Silvermist!" Fira said. "You're going to be late!"

"I know. But I promised Iris I would take something for her," Silvermist replied. "I'll just wait a bit longer."

Iris, a garden-talent fairy, wanted to bring flowers to the picnic. None of the other fairies thought that was necessary. After all, there would be all sorts of flowers growing on the island. But Iris had insisted.

"OK, Silvermist. But hurry," Fira said. "Right now is the perfect time for a picnic. It's almost high noon. The sun will be right over our heads."

Silvermist watched Fira join the others. Then she settled back and took in the scene. It all looked so lovely. The canoes drifted in rows while the fairies flew gracefully above. Silvermist didn't want to miss any of the picnic. *But if I'm going to be late anyway,* she thought, *I may as well relax.*

"Silvermist! Silvermist!" Iris rushed up with an armful of messy-looking wildflowers. As usual, her long narrow nose was red at the tip. "Here I am!"

She stood the flowers at the back of the canoe. "Whew! That took a while. But I knew you wouldn't leave before I got here!"

Silvermist glanced over at the flowers. "What are they?"

"They are very rare chrysanthe-poppies. I searched every field in Pixie Hollow just to find them."

"Chrysanthe-poppies?" Silvermist had never heard of them.

"Here, I'll show you!" Iris flipped open her huge book about flowers.

Iris was the only garden fairy who didn't have her own garden. Instead, she put all her energy into writing her plant book. She claimed to be an expert on every plant, flower, and seed in Never Land.

Silvermist examined the flowers. Honestly, they looked more like weeds than anything else. But taking these flowers to the picnic meant a lot to Iris. So Silvermist was happy to help her.

"I'm going now!" Iris said as she flew away. "Don't bump the canoe too much, Silvermist. The flowers are very delicate!"

Silvermist paddled away from the shore. Most of the other fairies were already on the island. But the day was so beautiful, Silvermist decided to take her time and enjoy the trip.

"Moving a bit slowly today, sweetheart?" asked Vidia, a fast-flying fairy, as she landed lightly on the end of Silvermist's canoe.

Vidia gave Silvermist her usual

smirk. It showed a mix of scorn and boredom. Vidia always acted as if she had someplace better to be and somebody better to be with.

"Are you going to the picnic?" Silvermist asked, though she already knew the answer. Vidia didn't bother much with fairy gatherings.

"Me?" Vidia laughed. "Goodness, no. I just happened to be flying by, and I saw all these fairies happily picnicking on the island. You, however, sweetie, seem to have... ahem... missed the boat. I thought water fairies were skilled at paddling. Are you feeling all right?" Vidia's voice was full of fake concern.

"I'm fine, Vidia," Silvermist said. She was nearing the island. Fira waved to her from the shore.

"Fine?" Vidia repeated. "There's nothing fine about going at a snail's pace. I've never seen a water fairy paddle so slowly."

Silvermist just shrugged. She continued to move at the same speed.

Vidia frowned. Usually she could get a rise out of fairies. But her words had no effect on Silvermist. "Whatever could be – "

"How are my flowers doing?" Iris shouted to Silvermist from the water's edge.

"Flowers? Is that what those weeds are?" Vidia leaned over to peer at the untidy bundle.

The canoe tipped.

"Oh!" Vidia cried. Her feet slipped out from under her, and she fell backwards. Her wings dipped into the stream. They soaked up water like a sea sponge. Try as she might, Vidia couldn't find her balance again.

Vidia fell into the water with a loud splash.

"Help! Help!" Iris shouted. "My picnic flowers are ruined. And Vidia's drowning!"

2

VIDIA FLAILED IN the stream. The water continued to seep into her wings, dragging her down.

"Hang on, Vidia! I'll get you!" Silvermist cried. She dropped to her knees and reached out.

Vidia waved her arms in alarm. "Calm down!" Silvermist shouted. "I can't get hold of you!"

"Help! Help!" Iris shrieked loudly from the shore.

A crowd of fairies flew over. Quickly, they pulled Vidia out of the water.

"Look at this!" Rani said. She waded into the stream. "It's not deep at all! The water doesn't even reach up to my waist!"

Sitting on the sandy beach, Vidia

glared at Rani. Her glow turned bright red.

"That's a good joke on you, Vidia," Prilla said with a giggle. "You could have just stood up!"

Silvermist's canoe bumped against the shore. She climbed out.

"Shush, everyone!" Silvermist hurried over to Vidia. "Are you all right?" she asked.

Silvermist's heartfelt concern seemed to annoy Vidia even more than the teasing did.

"I'm f-f-fine," Vidia said. Her teeth chattered. She was shivering from the cool water. "I was balancing p-p-perfectly well. But then you had to squirm around and rock the boat."

"How can you blame Silvermist?" Tink asked.

Vidia raised her eyebrows. "Oh, please! I d-d-didn't arrive yesterday. You don't think I'd just fall in, d-d-do you?"

"Accidents happen," Silvermist said.

"Not to me," Vidia snapped. She glared at the surrounding fairies. "Why don't you go back to your l-l-little picnic!"

Fira shrugged and wandered away with the other fairies. Only Silvermist remained. "Do you need a blanket?" she asked. "Or something to eat?"

Vidia shook her dripping wings. Then she stood and drew herself up to her full five inches.

"If I could, Silvermist, sweetheart, I'd f-f-fly away right now. But since I'm stuck at this s-s-s-silly picnic until my wings dry, I'll manage fine."

Vidia tossed her long, wet ponytail and turned away.

Silvermist sat with Fira and Tinker Bell. She ate berries and tiny watercress sandwiches. Every now and then, she glanced over at Vidia.

She felt terrible about what had happened. No fairy liked to have water-logged wings. And she knew that Vidia hated to be made fun of. Still, Silvermist found herself enjoying the picnic.

As soon as she finished eating, clean-up talents whisked away her plate. Fira stood up and said, "We have hours before sunset. What should we do?"

Beck, an animal-talent fairy, jumped to her feet. "I know! Let's play spots and dots!" she said.

Silvermist smiled. She hadn't played that game in a while.

Beck cupped her hands around her mouth like a megaphone. Then she made a loud clicking noise with her tongue.

A moment later, dozens of ladybugs flew to her side. She whispered to the bugs. She was making sure they wanted to play.

"Now, does everyone remember the rules?" she asked the fairies. "We give the ladybugs ten seconds to hide. You have to find as many ladybugs as you can and count the dots on their backs. Whoever scores highest wins!"

She handed out lily pads and berry-ink pens to record the spots and dots. "Ready?"

"Ready!" shouted everyone but Vidia. "Count!"

Silvermist began counting slowly with the others. "One Pixie Hollow. Two Pixie Hollow. Three..." As they counted, the ladybugs flew off to hide.

As soon as the fairies and sparrow men reached ten, they darted away. They flew here and there, trying to find as many ladybugs as they could.

Silvermist trailed the others. She wasn't in a hurry. She checked every hiding place... every nook... every cranny. She looked under every leaf and behind every rock.

She found one ladybug between the roots of a hickory tree, and another in the dense branches of a mulberry bush. A third was hiding in a bird's nest.

Silvermist sat under a shady leaf to add up her points. *Wait a minute!* she thought. She saw a silhouette through the leaf. It was shaped like a ladybug!

This could be it – the one that would give her more points than any other fairy! She stepped away from the leaf for a better look.

It *was* a ladybug. But it was the strangest ladybug Silvermist had ever seen. It was milky white, from tip to tip.

Its spots were difficult to see. They were white, too, just a shade darker than the rest of the ladybug – and there must have been a dozen of them!

She'd found a ladybug with the most dots she'd ever counted! Surely, she'd win the game.

Silvermist looked down to tally her

score. As she did, the white ladybug hopped onto her head.

"Hey!" she called out to the other fairies. "Do I get extra points if a ladybug finds *me*?"

Beck and Fawn hurried over. "A white ladybug!" Beck peered up at the insect. "I've never seen one before!"

"It's very rare," Fawn agreed.

By now, other fairies had gathered around Silvermist. The ladybug sat perfectly still atop the water-talent fairy's head.

"You know," a garden fairy named Rosetta mused, "there's an old superstition about white ladybugs. They're supposed to bring – "

"Bad luck!" Iris said, screeching to a stop in front of Silvermist.

A few fairies chuckled uncertainly. No one took Iris very seriously. But fairies were superstitious creatures. They believed in wishes, charms, and luck – both good and bad.

"The white ladybug!" Iris's voice rose higher and higher. "It's cursed!"

3

A HUSH FELL over the picnic site. All around Silvermist, fairies stopped playing. They stopped talking. They even stopped moving.

Silvermist shook her head. She hoped the ladybug would fly away. But it didn't. It just settled more comfortably in place.

"Oh, this is bad," Iris moaned. "A cursed white ladybug. Make it go away!"

A murmur went through the crowd. Some fairies gasped.

"Stop that, Iris!" Fira spoke sharply. "You're scaring everyone."

"She's not *scaring* me," Silvermist said. "But going around with a ladybug on my head will be a bother."

"Here, let us help." Beck flew closer, with Fawn by her side. Gently, they lifted the bug and carried it to a tree.

The ladybug paused for a moment. Then it flew up and disappeared among the leaves.

"Well." Silvermist looked around at the other fairies. "That was a little strange."

Iris backed away from her. She had a wild look in her eye. "It's not just strange, Silvermist. It's bad, as in bad luck. A white ladybug is bad luck. And to have one land on your head? That's the worst possible luck."

Slowly, the fairies turned to one another. Their voices were hushed but urgent. "Silvermist has been touched by a white ladybug!" "It's bad luck!" "She's cursed!"

Silvermist couldn't believe it. Everyone was scared of a harmless ladybug? And why? Because of a foolish myth?

Silvermist shrugged. "I don't really believe in those old fairy superstitions."

She smiled at Fira and her other friends. She was expecting to see nods of agreement. She thought they'd say, "Yes, we know exactly what you mean." Instead, everyone was silent. The island was quiet, too. No birds cooed. No bees buzzed.

Everyone stared at Silvermist. They had frightened looks on their faces. Finally, Fira spoke. "I don't know, Silvermist..."

Iris's nose turned even redder than usual. "What's not to know?" she shouted. "Everyone saw it!

Right on Silvermist's head!"

"Let's stay calm," Rani said. She sounded nervous, though. "Let's not think the worst."

"I'm not thinking any such thing. And I *am* calm," Silvermist said in a level voice. "There's no such thing as bad luck."

Humidia wiped away a tear. "Are you sure?" she asked weepily.

"Yes, I'm sure. The curse means nothing. It's an old fairy tale… like 'step on a crack, break a sparrow man's back.' Right, Terence?"

"Right!" the dust-talent sparrow man said, a little too quickly. He thumped himself on the back. "Not one broken bone!"

"So!" Silvermist grinned at her

friends. "I'm not going to pay attention to this crazy superstition. And neither should anyone else."

"The curse is real!" Iris insisted. "Why, back when I had my own garden..."

Everyone sighed. Iris was always going on about the good old days, when she had the most amazing garden in all of Pixie Hollow. They were tired of hearing it. They turned away.

"Maybe we should go back to the Home Tree," Terence suggested. "You could get some rest, Silvermist."

"Yes," Rani agreed. "You must be feeling... strange."

Everyone else is acting *strange,* Silvermist thought. She felt just as she always did. And she'd been having such fun.

She didn't want it to end.

"Really, I'm fine," she told the others.

Fira stepped forward. "Do you know what I think?"

Silvermist caught her breath. Fira looked serious. Did she believe in the curse, too?

"I think we should play fairy tag," Fira finished.

Silvermist smiled. She knew she could count on her friend.

"So you want to play?" Tink asked.

"Of course!" Silvermist said.

"Then…" Fira tapped Silvermist on the head. "Choose you!"

"Water talents are chosen!" Rani declared.

For a moment, no one moved. Not even Silvermist. Then she fluttered a wing.

Fairies scattered in all directions.

The water talents dashed here and there, trying to tag fairies from different talents.

Silvermist hovered above the beach. *Let's see*, she thought. *Which fairy should I tag?*

She spied Beck just a short distance away. Beck was flying around a beehive. She wasn't looking behind her.

"This should be easy!" Silvermist said to herself. All thoughts of the white ladybug and the curse were already far from her mind.

She neared the beehive just as Beck swung around.

Beck laughed. She had nowhere to go. Tree branches blocked her every move. Quickly, she flew into a knothole.

"You can't escape that way, Beck!" Silvermist called playfully. She flew after her friend.

"Yoo-hoo, Silvermist!" Fawn called. "What about me?"

"Fawn?" Silvermist turned her head. And in that split second, she missed the knothole and crashed right into the tree trunk.

"Ouch!" She fluttered to the ground.

"Hurry! Hurry!" Fawn cried. "We need healing talents. Now!"

Silvermist rubbed her forehead. Already, a pea-sized bump was forming on it.

"Do you need a leaf compress? An icy-water pack?" asked Clara, the first healing talent to arrive.

Silvermist tried to shake her head.

"Ouch!" she said again. "Well, maybe the pack," she admitted. Clara handed her a pink petal-pouch full of water. Silvermist held it in her hand for a moment, helping the pack freeze. Then Clara placed the icy pack on the bump.

"Are you all right?" Fira asked, landing beside Silvermist. "What happened to you?"

"I'm fine, Fira. I just missed a knothole and hit the tree instead."

Fira lifted the pack to check the bump. "That doesn't look fine to me." She lowered her voice. "Do you... do you think it could be the curse?"

"No, Fira. I don't." Silvermist spoke in an even tone. "It was just an accident. A regular, everyday sort of accident. Like I told Vidia, accidents happen.

Any fairy could have done it."

"Any fairy?" Vidia flew over. Her wings were finally dry. She circled above everyone and shot a triumphant look at Silvermist. Her glow had lost its embarrassed pink tinge. She tossed her head, proud as ever.

"Any fairy would fly right into a big old tree? I don't think so." Vidia clucked with false concern. "No, sweetie, a fairy needs to be pretty unlucky to do that."

4

UNLUCKY? SILVERMIST DIDN'T feel unlucky, despite what Vidia said. Any fairy could have a little flying accident. Any fairy could turn her head for just an instant and fly into something, even a tree.

"It's nothing to worry about," she told herself. "There is no curse."

Still, she knew that the other fairies were whispering. They were saying she'd had bad luck. They were saying she was cursed.

But I don't believe it, Silvermist thought. *Not now. Not ever.*

The picnic wasn't over yet, but Silvermist didn't feel like returning to it. Instead, she flew to the seashore to watch the ocean waves. She wanted to be alone. She didn't want to hear the fairy gossip.

Hours passed. When the tide went out, it left small pools of water scattered around the shore. Silvermist flew from tidal pool to tidal pool, looking for hermit crabs and tiny fish.

Then something caught her eye. A sparkling object was lying on the beach. Was it a shiny rock? A piece of sea glass? She flitted closer. It was a seashell! The tiniest, most perfect shell she'd ever seen.

Silvermist picked it up. Its inside was orange with wavy lines that spread out like rays of sunshine. Silvermist knew that it was special. Just holding it made her feel better.

Let the fairies and sparrow men talk

of curses and bad luck. She didn't care.

She slipped the shell into a fold of her dress and flew back towards the Home Tree.

When she got there, Silvermist flew on to the tearoom. It was empty. Next door, in the kitchen, baking and cooking talents were hard at work, preparing the evening meal.

Silvermist was too early for dinner. But maybe she could help in the kitchen. She would see if the cooking fairies needed help boiling water.

She ducked through the swinging door. Fairies flitted around the room, mixing, beating, sprinkling, and stirring. Two sparrow men stood by the sink, rinsing dirt off a big carrot.

"Dulcie!" Silvermist called.

"Is there anything I can do?"

Dulcie was kneading dough at the big table in the centre of the room. "Well, I don't know," she said, a little uneasily. "Are you feeling OK? Is your bump all healed?"

"All better," Silvermist declared.

"That's good. But there's really nothing for you to do here, Silvermist." Dulcie nodded at the stove. Three pots of water were already boiling merrily. "You don't even have to come inside. Really."

She's nervous about my being here, Silvermist realised. *She's afraid I'll bring bad luck or have another accident. I have to show her that nothing has changed. I'm the same water fairy I've always been.*

"What about those pitchers?" she

asked. Rows of water pitchers lined a long table across the room from the sink. "I could fill them for you."

"I don't think– " Dulcie began.

But Silvermist was already at the water pump. She caught the water as it flowed. Then, with a gentle underhand toss, she sent it streaming over Dulcie's head and into the first pitcher.

Not one drop spilled.

"See?" Silvermist grinned triumphantly. "I can do this quickly, while the carrot is being washed."

On the other side of the swinging doors, fairies were heading into the tearoom for dinner. "Well, it *would* help move things along," Dulcie admitted.

At that moment, Vidia swept into the kitchen. "I was just flying past. You know, normally I like to dine alone. But I saw you here, Silvermist, and I had to drop in and see how you were."

"Oh?" Silvermist concentrated on the next pitcher of water.

"Yes." Vidia made herself comfortable in a chair next to Dulcie. "You were at the picnic, weren't you, Dulcie, dear? So you know about poor Silvermist and the ladybug?"

Dulcie nodded.

"Well, I just wanted to make sure she hadn't had any other" – Vidia paused to make sure she had Silvermist's full attention – "unfortunate accidents."

"Nope." Silvermist shot another expert stream into the next pitcher. "Not one."

Vidia gave her a tight-lipped smile.

"Good," she said. She sounded as if she meant the opposite. "Although, not much time has passed, really. Anything could happen. You know, you can't ignore the magic behind these old tales. Just the other day, I heard about a butterfly herder. He forgot to cross his wings before passing the skeleton tree..."

Dulcie had stopped working. She turned to Vidia, taking in every word. The other fairies and sparrow men leaned closer, straining to hear.

"... and the next thing he knew, his entire herd of butterflies had flown off. He never found them!" said Vidia.

Silvermist tried not to listen. She kept quietly filling pitchers.

"And there was that sparrow man who broke some sea glass," Vidia went

35

on. "He had seven hundred years of bad luck. At least that's what everyone thinks. But no one ever saw him after year five thirty-nine."

She stole a glance at Silvermist.

"And there was a garden-talent fairy who opened a petal umbrella inside the Home Tree. Well, right after that, she planted a carrot seed – or so she thought. Turned out she'd planted the seed of a snareweed plant. When the thing sprouted, it nearly ate her!"

Silvermist's hands were steady as she worked. She stayed calm, even as Vidia's stories grew more and more outrageous. But really, she couldn't wait to finish. All that talk about bad luck and curses! She wanted it to end.

"I'm done," Silvermist said. She

crossed the kitchen to check the water level in the pitchers. "Looks OK to me," she announced. "What do you think, Dulcie?"

"Perfect!" Dulcie declared.

"See? Not one accident," Silvermist couldn't resist saying to Vidia. "I guess I'll go into the tearoom now."

Silvermist turned. Her wing brushed against a pitcher. The pitcher tipped andfell against another pitcher. Then that pitcher tipped, knocking over a third that fell against a fourth that tumbled into a fifth.

Silvermist tried to catch them, but she wasn't quick enough. Pitcher after pitcher toppled. And fast-flying Vidia didn't move a muscle to help. She just sat there, smiling.

Silvermist gazed at the kitchen.

Water had spilled everywhere. It had splashed onto the honey buns and into the walnut soup. It poured over plates and cups and across the floor. Fairies rushed around the room with moss mops and towels.

"Hmmm," Vidia said. "Looks like dinner might be late tonight. What do you think, Silvermist?"

5

THE TEAROOM WAS filled with fairies and sparrow men. Each one stared at the swinging doors to the kitchen. They were all waiting for dinner.

Dulcie flew through the kitchen doors. "The meal will be served late," she announced.

At the water-talent table, Silvermist ducked her head. She knew that it was her fault dinner was late.

But Dulcie and the others will work their kitchen magic, she thought. *Everyone will be eating delicious food in no time.* There was no reason to be upset.

Minutes later, the serving talents brought out steaming bowls of acorn soup and sunflower stew. It *was* delicious. Silvermist had been right. The accident wasn't anything to worry about. Not really.

Just then, Vidia flew to the fast-flying-talent table. She was so rarely in the tearoom that she had nowhere to sit. "No, no, don't get up," she said, even though no one was offering a chair. "I'm not staying, darlings. I just wanted to make sure those gossipy serving talents weren't spreading any rumours."

The serving talents stopped their work to look at Vidia. Not one of them had been talking. They'd been moving so quickly to serve dinner, they hadn't had time to say a word.

Now all eyes were on Vidia.

Vidia cast a look at Silvermist, making sure everyone noticed. "I wouldn't want any fairy to be the subject of idle gossip," she went on. "But…" She stretched out the word meaningfully.

Iris leaped to her feet. "Something happened to Silvermist! I knew it! What, Vidia? Was it another accident?"

Fairies and sparrow men swiveled in their seats to stare at Silvermist.

"I'll answer that." Silvermist's voice was steady. "I spilled some water, Iris. It was just a little spill."

"Is that what you'd call it, darling?" Vidia asked.

A voice rang out from the kitchen. "Clean-up talents! We need help in the pantry! The flour is soaked! The spices are drenched! The fruit is soggy! It's a mess!"

Silvermist looked calmly back at Vidia. She felt bad about causing the mess. But really, the whole idea of the curse was so silly. Why not make a joke of it?

"Maybe I *would* call it a little spill," she answered Vidia with a laugh. "And maybe I'd call Torth Mountain an anthill."

Across the room, Fira chuckled. "And maybe the sun is just a firefly torch," she added.

"And the Home Tree is a little sapling," said Rosetta.

Soon, everyone was joining in the game. It seemed they'd all forgotten about the accident.

Silvermist kept thinking about it, though. An image flashed through her mind: pitcher after pitcher falling over.

Yes, she'd managed to laugh off the spill. But what about her flying accident?

Was there something to what Vidia had said? Did the old fairy tales have a powerful magic?

She glanced at Vidia, who was standing by the fast-flying table. She looked like she knew what Silvermist was thinking. Vidia gave her a slow, cruel smile. And with a flick of her ponytail, she flew out of the tearoom.

Dessert berries were on the tables now. Dinner would be over soon. Silvermist reached for the sugar bowl.

"Oops!" She knocked over the pepper shaker. The top popped off. Pepper scattered across the table. Silvermist hoped no one had noticed. But no such luck.

"Oh!" Iris moaned. "Spilled pepper? That's bad luck, too!"

"Quick!" Fira said. "Toss some over your left shoulder!"

Silvermist scooped up a handful of pepper. Without thinking, she threw it over her shoulder... right into the face of a serving talent who was carrying a platter of almond pudding.

"Watch out!" Rosetta cried. But it was too late.

The serving talent sneezed. The platter flipped. Pudding flew everywhere.

Another disaster, Silvermist thought with a groan.

It seemed that all the fairies and sparrow men had lost their appetites. One by one, they filed quietly out of the tearoom.

Fira stopped to give Silvermist a quick hug.

"I'll just sit here a little longer," Silvermist told her. Fira nodded and went on her way.

Alone and confused, Silvermist sighed. The tree and water accidents weren't as easy to explain away any more. Not after the pepper mishap.

Maybe I truly am unlucky, she thought. *Maybe the curse is real.*

6

Silvermist felt better after a good night's sleep. In the morning light, the talk of bad luck seemed silly.

She flung open her window to let in the fresh air.

Chirp, ch-ch-chirp! A cricket hopped onto a branch outside her window. He rubbed his back legs together, chirping.

The music was so sweet, so soothing. Silvermist smiled. *The cricket is singing just for me,* she thought.

Silvermist sat down next to the window. She listened to the cricket for a long time.

If she were really unlucky, would this be happening? Would a cricket give her a private concert?

With one final chirp, the cricket hopped away.

Humming his song under her breath, Silvermist flew out to the courtyard. It seemed every fairy and sparrow man in Pixie Hollow was returning from somewhere.

"Wasn't that amazing?" asked Fawn, rushing over to Silvermist. "If I tried, I couldn't organise a concert like that."

Does Fawn mean the cricket by my window? Silvermist wondered. *But how would she know about that?*

"All those songbirds," Fawn went on. "There must have been thirty of them! All singing so sweetly. It was like nothing I've ever heard. Why they landed in the fairy circle to sing, I'll never know."

Beck joined them. "I don't think we'll see something like that again. Not for years and years – if ever!"

Slowly, Silvermist began to understand. There had been a songbird concert. An unexpected, wonderful performance, the likes of which no one had heard before. And she'd missed it.

Suddenly, Silvermist's private concert didn't seem so special. She didn't feel very lucky at all.

"Oh, Silvermist!" Fira rushed over. "You weren't there!"

"I know." If only she had woken up sooner, she might have seen the concert. Wouldn't anything go right for her?

Just then, she remembered something that *had* gone right. "Wait a minute!" she said to Fira. "I have something to show you!"

Her special seashell. The one she'd found on the beach. Just remembering it made Silvermist feel better. She reached into the fold of her dress.

It was empty. "Oh!" she gasped. "Where is it?" She felt around every inch of the fabric.

One of her fingers poked out through the bottom.

Her dress had a hole. The seashell had fallen out, Silvermist realised. She could search and search, but what good would it do? She'd never find it.

She wasn't the kind of fairy who found lost things any more. She was the kind of fairy who flew into trees. And tipped over water pitchers. And ruined desserts. And missed songbirds.

Silvermist *was* unlucky. She was

cursed. There was no doubt about it.

Word spread quickly through the Home Tree. Silvermist had missed the best concert in Pixie Hollow history – just because she had been late!

"I told you! I told you! She's cursed!" Iris said, fluttering from fairy to fairy.

With Iris moaning and crying, everyone looked worried. It was hard for Silvermist to stay calm. Her glow flared bright orange with embarrassment.

"Ahem!" Rani cleared her throat. "I have an announcement to make," she said, thinking quickly. Fairies shifted their attention. Silvermist's glow faded. She smiled at Rani gratefully.

"There will be a waterball tournament in two days," Rani said. "All are welcome to watch. And all water talents are invited to show their skills."

A waterball tournament! Silvermist loved contests. She enjoyed matching throws with her friends and aiming waterballs at targets. But she couldn't do it now. With her luck, the tournament would be a disaster.

"I'll be there!" Humidia declared.

"So will I!" another water talent called out.

"I'm sure Silvermist won't be taking part," Vidia said, "due to a severe case of bad luck."

What? Silvermist turned to frown at her. Vidia couldn't speak for her! True, she'd been thinking the very same thing.

But for Vidia to say what she should do… well, that was unacceptable!

"Vidia is mistaken," Silvermist said. "I will be there." She smiled at Rani.

The water talents cheered. Silvermist knew she had done the right thing.

There was only one problem. Like Vidia had said, anything could happen.

7

"Oh, why did I say I'd do it?" Silvermist asked Fira. She felt funny. Nervous and uneasy. And to be honest, she even felt a little panicky. For Silvermist, this was strange indeed.

"Why did I ever say I'd be in the tournament?" Silvermist moaned. "I just know something's going to go terribly wrong."

Silvermist and Fira were leaving the courtyard. "We'll think of something," Fira said as they flew through the halls of the Home Tree.

"Hey! Wait!" The light-talent fairy skidded to a stop in front of the Home Tree library. "Let's go in here. The library has lots of books on superstitions. It might give us an idea."

Well, Silvermist thought, *it's better than doing nothing.*

"OK," she agreed.

Inside, Fira led Silvermist to a far corner. A small sign read LUCK: GOOD AND BAD. The entire section – bookcase after bookcase – held books about superstition.

"I never knew this was here," said Silvermist .

"Of course not," Fira replied. "You never thought to look."

Fira brought Silvermist to a shelf marked Bugs and Insects. Silvermist flipped open one book. It had two chapters on the rare white ladybug. The next book had three chapters. And another was simply titled Beware the White Ladybug.

Silvermist began to read.

"'Good-luck charms and bad-luck curses are all around us. And perhaps the most powerful of all, is the curse cast by the white ladybug.'"

Silvermist gasped. Most powerful? A lump formed in her throat. "Oh, Fira. It's the worst curse of all. What can I do? It's hopeless!"

Fira leaped up to comfort her. "It doesn't have to be hopeless! Look at all these other books."

Fira pulled another book off the shelf. The title was *Never Bad Luck/ Always Good Luck*.

"You mean, I might be able to undo the curse with a good-luck charm?" Silvermist asked.

Fira grinned at her friend. "Let's find out!"

Silvermist and Fira read through the night. By early the next morning, they had put together a list called Things to Do to Bring Good Luck.

Silvermist sighed. "Do you think I can really drive away the curse?"

"Of course! We just have to find the right charm," Fira said.

Silvermist read the first good-luck charm on the list. "'Circle the Home Tree counterclockwise seven times under a blue moon.' When is the next blue moon?" she asked.

"Next year," Fira told her.

Silvermist crossed that item off the list. She'd have to try another one. "Ok, number two: 'Find a five-leaf clover.'"

Silvermist pictured all the fields and meadows in Pixie Hollow. Surely, there must be a five-leaf clover hidden with in them. But how long would it take to check all those places? The tournament was the next day. It seemed too risky.

She read the next item on the list. "'Spot a triple rainbow.'"

It was a bright, sunny day. There was little chance of seeing any rainbow, let alone a triple one.

Finally, she read, "'Find a pin and pick it up.'"

"That sounds simple," Fira said. "Sewing talents are always using pins."

"Right," Silvermist agreed. "Let's find a sewing fairy, then."

"And ask her for a pin?"

Silvermist thought for a moment, then shook her head. "That wouldn't exactly be finding one, would it?"

"What if we follow her," Fira suggested, "and if she drops one, you can pick it up!"

Silvermist grinned. "And get good luck!"

The two friends hurried from the library. They circled the lobby and the tearoom. But it was early. Hardly anyone was about. They didn't see a single sewing talent.

They flew up to the floor where most of the sewing talents had their rooms.

Just then, Hem fluttered into the hallway. Silvermist nudged Fira and pointed. The pockets on Hem's sewing apron were stuffed with needles and pins.

"Time to check those spiderwebs," Hem was muttering. "See if they're clean and ready for the queen's gown."

"She's going to the laundry room," Fira hissed to Silvermist.

Hem flew down through the Home Tree, heading towards the lowest floor. Silvermist and Fira followed quietly.

On the sixth floor, Hem glanced over her left shoulder. In a flash, Silvermist and Fira ducked into a supply closet. Hem shrugged and continued on.

On the fourth floor, Hem glanced over her right shoulder. Silvermist and Fira scurried behind a big potted fern.

On the second floor, Hem whirled around. "Hello?" she called. "Anyone there?"

Silvermist and Fira leaped into a dark corner. They held their breath and waited. Finally, Silvermist poked out her head. Hem was gone. "All clear,"

Silvermist whispered to Fira.

They flew quickly to the laundry room. But Hem had stopped suddenly just inside the door. They almost bumped into her. Thinking fast, Silvermist and Fira dove into a laundry basket.

"Lympia, did you hear something?" Hem asked a laundry-talent fairy.

"Hmmm?" Lympia murmured. She wasn't paying attention. She was busy scrubbing leafkerchiefs in a washtub.

"I feel like somebody's following me," said Hem.

"Why would anyone follow you?" Lympia asked briskly. She handed Hem a pile of clean, neatly folded spiderwebs.

Hem shrugged.

Silvermist lifted her head out of the laundry basket. Just then, a pile of dirty dresses tumbled down a laundry chute, landing on her.

"Oh!" she yelped.

"There! Did you hear that?" Hem demanded.

But Lympia had turned away and was already sprinkling fairy dust on a stained spider-silk tablecloth.

Holding the spiderwebs, Hem flew out of the room. Silvermist and Fira climbed quietly out of the basket, scattering dresses every which way.

"Tut, tut," they heard Lympia say as they hurried after Hem. "Tinker Bell needs to check these chutes. They're shooting clothes in all directions!"

Hem turned a corner.

Silvermist and Fira turned a corner.

Hem flew into the courtyard.

Silvermist and Fira flew into the courtyard.

Hem was flying faster and faster. She dropped a spiderweb, but she didn't bother to pick it up. She kept glancing behind her with a worried expression.

Silvermist and Fira flew faster and faster, too. They dodged the threads of spiderweb Hem left in her wake. Silvermist watched for a dropped pin. But once again, she was out of luck.

Finally, Hem flew into the sewing room. She slammed the door behind her – right in Silvermist's face.

"Quick! Through the window!" Fira whispered.

They flew out a window in the hall. They darted around the outside of the

Home Tree and flew back in through a sewing-room window.

The workplace was abuzz with activity. Swiftly, Silvermist and Fira hid behind a wall tapestry. They were almost completely hidden. Only their feet stuck out from the bottom.

Silvermist peeked out from the side of the tapestry. One group of sewing talents sat in the middle of the floor. They were sorting pins into three piles: small, smaller, and smallest.

"I can't just pluck one from there," Silvermist whispered to Fira. "That wouldn't be finding it."

But then she spied something long and thin under a wicker chair in the corner. It was a pin! And she'd found it!

Hem was busy threading a needle.

Everyone else was sewing and sorting. This was Silvermist's chance. She sneaked out from behind the tapestry. She stayed close to the wall. Quietly... calmly... she stooped to pick up the pin. Then she stood – and came face to face with Hem.

"Aha!" Hem cried. She whipped the tapestry away from the wall, revealing Fira. The rest of the sewing talents stopped working and looked up in surprise. "I knew something funny was going on," said Hem.

Fira stepped into the centre of the room. "Nothing funny is going on. We just wanted to... uh... watch you, Hem. Your talent is so extraordinary. What skill it takes to thread a pine needle! Why, I could never do that!"

"Well!" Hem said, relaxing a bit. She was flattered. "You can visit anytime, Fira."

"Really? We can visit any time?" said Silvermist, smiling.

"We're very busy, preparing for the contest tomorrow," Hem said. She eyed Silvermist with concern. "Besides, we try to stay accident free here. You know, with so many sharp pins and needles around."

Silvermist understood. Just like Dulcie, Hem didn't want Silvermist anywhere near her workspace. Silvermist turned to leave.

"Just a minute," Hem said. "What's that you're holding?"

"It's uh... uh...," Silvermist stammered. "It's a pin." She opened her hand. "For luck."

Hem gave her a sad smile. "I wish I could help you, Silvermist. But we need every one of these pins to do our work."

Silvermist nodded. She walked over to the group of sorting fairies. She dropped the pin into the "smaller" pile.

"It's a 'smallest,'" Hem told her.

"Oh!" Silvermist bent to retrieve it.

"No, don't! I'll get it!" Hem cried. She lunged forward.

Startled, Silvermist jumped. She bumped into the piles of pins. Small, smaller, and smallest all scattered. They rolled under chairs, into cracks, and out the door.

Silvermist whirled around. "Don't worry. I'll pick them up!" she cried.

"No! No! That's OK, Silvermist!"

Hem said. "We'll take care of it."

Silvermist backed slowly out the door. In the hall, she tried to smile at Fira.

"That was a disaster," she said.

8

Fira led Silvermist outside. "Who needs a pin, anyway?" Fira said. "We have lots of other things on the good-luck list."

Fira took out the paper and read, "'Find the Circle Constellation in the night sky. The centre star winks once each night. When you see it wink, wish for luck.'"

"It's hours until sunset," Silvermist said. "What else?"

"'Find a swan feather.'"

"Hmmm." Silvermist thought out loud. "We'll have to find a swan first. I remember seeing a pair of swans swimming at Havendish Stream." She fluttered her wings. "Let's try that one!"

Havendish Stream was crowded with fairies and sparrow men. Some were washing their wings. Others picked flowers by the shore. But as they spotted Silvermist, they flew off one by one.

"Well, at least we have a clear view of the stream," Silvermist said. She was trying to look on the bright side.

The sparkling water and the sound of the waves lifted Silvermist's spirits. She flew from one end of the stream to the other. But she didn't spot a single swan.

She sighed. "The swans must have left. We'll have to try somewhere else. Somewhere outside Pixie Hollow." She looked at Fira. "This might take a while. Is that all right?"

Fira nodded. "I have to be back by dusk. The light talents are practicing a moonlight dance tonight. But it shouldn't take long to find one big swan."

The fairies set off. Silvermist hoped Never Land's magic would help her. Maybe the wind would guide them in the right direction. Or maybe the island would shrink so they wouldn't have far to fly.

But if anything, the island seemed to grow. Their route seemed to get longer. It took hours just to reach Gull Pond, right outside Pixie Hollow.

Seagulls dove around the pond. But there were no swans.

So Silvermist and Fira flew even farther from Pixie Hollow, to Wough River. The river was wide. The water was high and noisy. They flew back and forth over it. Each time they crossed, Silvermist was sure the river had stretched even wider.

No, Never Land wasn't helping. And luck certainly wasn't on her side.

"No swans here," Silvermist said with a sigh.

Finally, they came to Crescent Lake. They picked berries to snack on and sipped rainwater cupped in leaves.

Fira looked at the sun. "It's getting late. If we don't see a swan soon, we'll have to turn back."

"Look!" Silvermist cried. She pointed to the sky. "There are two now."

The swans flew past a nest built on the bank.

"Come on!" Fira took Silvermist by the hand. "Let's check there!"

The fairies landed in the nest, which was made from grass and twigs. They flitted from one end to the other, searching for a feather.

"No." Silvermist shook her head. "There aren't any here."

"That's OK." Fira flapped her wings harder. "We'll follow the swans, like we followed Hem. They're bound to lose at least one feather!"

Silvermist started to follow Fira. But something jerked her back. She turned and saw that her dress was snagged on a twig. She twisted to try to free herself. But the cloth was stuck tight. Of all the luck!

She heard a flutter of wings behind her. "Fira!" she called. "Come closer and – "

Silvermist turned, expecting to see Fira hovering next to her. Instead, she came face to eyeball with an enormous angry black swan.

"Oh!" Silvermist's heart beat fast.

The swan stared at her. Its beak was inches from her face. Clearly, it didn't like having a little fairy in its nest.

"Calm down," Silvermist said to herself. "Swans are beautiful, gentle creatures."

But this swan was huge and seemed menacing. Silvermist's heart was racing now. She grabbed her dress and pulled hard.

Rrrip! Silvermist's dress tore free.

Moments later, she and Fira hovered behind a tree, hidden from the swan. Silvermist took a deep breath. "That was close."

The swan had joined its mate. Now

they both circled lazily over the water. From a safe distance, they seemed lovely and majestic once again.

"Should we follow them?" Fira asked.

Silvermist shook her head. She'd had enough of swans for one day. Besides, the sun was low in the sky. The fairies had missed lunch and dinner.

"We should leave now," she told Fira. "Before it gets too late."

"You're right," Fira said. "I'm tired."

"Me too," Silvermist agreed quickly. Their fairy dust was wearing off. Her wings felt heavy, and they still had to fly home. It wasn't fair to make Fira keep searching, Silvermist thought.

As the fairies headed back to Pixie Hollow, the low sun vanished behind the trees. Fira turned up her glow.

But it was still hard to see.

"Is this the way?" Silvermist asked. She flew into a small thicket.

Fira struggled to shine more brightly. She squinted. "No!" she called. "That's the – "

Silvermist flew out of the bramble. She scratched her arms. "I know, I know. That's the patch of itchy ivy we passed earlier."

Silvermist was tired and uncomfortable. Her dress was dirty and torn. She flew the rest of the way home in silence.

Will I be doomed forever? she wondered. *And what if the curse gets worse?*

She had no idea what would happen next. She wanted to be the old calm, cool Silvermist everyone counted on. But how could she be when she was cursed?

When they reached the Home Tree entrance, Silvermist hugged Fira tightly. "At least you're back in time for your light practice," she told her friend. "And now that I know where the swans are, I can find a feather in the morning. Of course," she added, "I won't get so close next time!"

There! Just having a plan made Silvermist feel hopeful.

"Swan feathers?" Beck flew into the Home Tree as Fira flew out. She paused next to Silvermist. "I'm afraid you won't have any luck with that. It's not the molting season. Swans won't lose their feathers for months and months."

All that trouble for nothing! thought Silvermist. And now she didn't have a plan after all. What if she was cursed forever?

9

FIRA HAD GONE to light-talent practice. Beck had gone to her room. Pixie Hollow was quiet. Silvermist stood by the Home Tree, unsure of what to do.

If she went to sleep, would she fall out of bed and break a wing? If she flew to the dairy barn, would she turn the milk sour? If she went to the fairy-dust mill, would the dust blow away with the wind?

Would disaster follow anywhere she went?

The waterball contest was early in the morning. If she wanted to be in it – if she wanted to end her streak of bad luck – she had to keep searching. She had to find good luck somewhere.

She scratched one itchy elbow, then

the other. Then she looked up at the night sky.

The night sky! She could search for the Circle Constellation.

Slowly and carefully, she made her way to the Never Land beach. Here, she had the soothing sounds of the waves and the greatest view of the stars.

Silvermist shivered. The night air was chilly. She found a leaf to wrap herself in. Then she settled against a rock and tilted her chin up to the sky.

Bright lights dotted the darkness. Silvermist had never really paid attention to the stars before. But now she could see that they grouped together in patterns that almost made pictures.

Do they always look like this? she wondered. Something seemed different.

Then she realised that the constellations were changing shape.

She thought she spied the Circle Constellation, but it changed into a square. An arrow shape turned into a snake. A leaf turned into a feather.

Was that how the stars always were? Maybe her eyes were fooling her. Or maybe this was more bad luck. Were the stars playing tricks, just the way the Wough River had been when it had widened as she'd tried to cross it?

Silvermist felt more determined than ever. She could wait until the stars tired of their game. She'd be patient. She was good at that.

Minutes ticked by. Silvermist kept staring at the sky. Her eyes began to ache from the strain. She was afraid to blink, afraid she'd miss the winking star. Still, she waited.

Suddenly, the stars froze in place. Silvermist leaped to her feet. There, to the left, was the Circle Constellation. She was sure of it. Right in the middle was one star. The star that would wink.

Silvermist held her breath. Would it happen now?

Yes! The star flashed once, off and on. She squeezed her eyes shut and said, "I wish for all my bad luck to end."

She opened her eyes and sighed with relief. She'd done it. She'd reversed the curse.

Now the stars were moving once again. They floated closer to the ground, and closer still.

All at once, Silvermist understood.

The bright lights weren't stars at all. They were light-talent fairies practicing their dance.

"That's what confused me." For a moment, Silvermist closed her eyes and pictured the changing shapes. "I guess I just wanted to believe so much…"

Her voice trailed off. She didn't have the strength to finish the sentence. A lone tear fell from her eye, then another and another. Soon Silvermist's tears flowed faster and faster.

Silvermist – the water-talent fairy who hardly ever cried – was sobbing.

Silvermist spent that night alone on the beach. She was afraid to go back to her room. With all those clouds in the sky, a storm could be brewing. She didn't want to attract the storm to the Home Tree.

If anything happened here at the beach, she'd be the only one in danger.

She slept fitfully. She meant to wake up early to search for another good-luck charm. Even though finding one seemed impossible, she wanted to keep trying. But her deepest sleep came after sunrise. And she was so tired from flying and searching. She didn't stir until she heard a voice.

"Good morning, darling."

Silvermist opened her eyes. Vidia was sitting next to her on the sand.

"You seem to have overslept," Vidia continued. "Good thing I decided to be your own personal wake-up fairy. I would never want you to miss an important event like the waterball contest."

Silvermist sat up. She rubbed her eyes.

"The tournament begins in ten minutes, sweetie. Everyone is expecting you," said Vidia.

"I don't think anyone wants me there. Fairies fly in the other direction when they see me coming now."

"That may be. Really, who could blame them?" Vidia paused. "But Queen Clarion announced at breakfast that she expects the game to go on as planned, with you playing, darling. It seems she wants life in Pixie Hollow to continue as if nothing's changed."

Silvermist took a deep breath. If Queen Clarion needed her to be there, she'd be there. Besides, she had told everyone she'd be in the contest. And she always kept her word.

"I'm ready," she said.

"Good." Vidia brushed the sand from her leggings. "This is one event I wouldn't want to miss."

10

By the time Silvermist got to the contest field, everything was already in place. Hem and the other sewing talents had finished a beautiful new gown for Queen Clarion. Celebration setup fairies had carefully moved the spiderweb target to one end of the field. And fairies from all talents had come to watch.

Queen Clarion sat on a large colourful mat near the targets. The other fairies and sparrow men milled about, talking and laughing.

As Silvermist walked past, Hem drew in her breath. "She's here," Hem hissed to another sewing talent. "Hold on to your pins!"

Heads turned. Wings fluttered. One by

one, the fairies edged away from Silvermist.

But Fira made her way over. "It will be OK," she told her friend. "Maybe your luck is turning."

"I don't think so," Silvermist said quietly. On the way to the contest, she'd picked up a leftover muffin from the tearoom. Before she could take one bite, she'd dropped it in a mud puddle.

"Fairies and sparrow men!" Queen Clarion said, clapping her hands. The crowd quieted. "Water talents, take your places behind the marked line. Everyone else, be seated. The competition is about to begin!"

Fira hurried off to join the other light talents. Silvermist walked slowly towards the water fairies, who were forming a line. Maybe no one would notice her if she stayed at the back.

Queen Clarion reminded everyone of the rules. "Each water talent will get five tries to hit the target. Those who do best will go on to the next set of targets."

Rani stood at a line drawn in the dirt. She stared at the spiderweb target and the bull's-eye circle in its centre. Then she dipped her hand into a bucket of water. She patted the water into a smooth ball. Winding up her arm, she pitched the waterball at the target.

The ball hit the spiderweb, close to the bull's-eye. The crowd cheered.

Water talent after water talent tried the game, until only Silvermist was left.

Hesitantly, she stepped forward. She scooped up the water, then stole a glance at Vidia. Silvermist wound up and made the throw.

The waterball soared through the air. It went up, up, up, then down, down, down.

Silvermist held her breath. The waterball was going towards the target. It was heading right for it. It was going to hit –

The waterball hit Queen Clarion full in the face.

Everyone gasped. Queen Clarion was soaked from head to toe. Water dripped from her hair and her dress. A puddle formed by her feet. Helper fairies hurried over with moss towels.

Silvermist could barely look. What had she done? And what would the queen do now?

To Silvermist's amazement, Queen Clarion… laughed!

"Well, that cooled me off!" said the queen. She wrung out her hair. Water drops flew everywhere, sprinkling the nearby fairies.

The queen laughed harder. Then Prilla clapped her hands and giggled. Tinker Bell chuckled. Soon everyone was laughing – everyone but Silvermist.

Queen Clarion took off one shoe and turned it over. A stream of water poured out.

Finally, Silvermist began to laugh. And the longer she laughed, the harder she laughed. Queen Clarion pouring water out of her shoe! The idea of it!

"Oh, oh." Silvermist laughed so hard her stomach hurt. She bent over, her arms hugging her sides.

And then she saw a five-leaf clover, right by her feet. A lucky clover.

"Rosetta!" Silvermist called. "Come

see this! Fira! Tink! Everyone! Look!"

Fairies crowded around Silvermist. The clover was beautiful, slender but strong. Silvermist felt stronger too. Finally, she'd found a good-luck charm.

"Is it all right to pick it?" she asked.

Iris rushed over, her plant book already open. "'Five-leaf clovers are meant to be picked,'" she read out loud. "'Their magic keeps them alive forever.'"

"They're magic – and lucky!" Fira added.

Gently, Silvermist tugged the clover from the ground. She held it in her hand, examining it carefully.

"This isn't a flower show," Vidia said with a yawn. "It's still your turn, Silvermist."

The contest! Silvermist had forgotten all about it. She tucked the clover behind her ear.

"Don't get rattled now, darling," Vidia called from her seat on a branch. Her voice was syrupy. "Finding a clover is all well and good. But how can it compete with a powerful curse?"

Silvermist gazed steadily at Vidia. *Rattled*, she thought. *That's exactly what Vidia wants me to be. Ever since Vidia fell in the water, she's wanted to get back at me. Every chance she's got, she's tried to upset me.*

So was that what the accidents had been about? Not a curse... or even bad luck. Just Silvermist making mistakes because she had felt flustered and unsure?

I don't know! she thought. But did it matter?

For the first time in a long while, Silvermist was thinking clearly. And that was when she remembered something else – the seashell she'd lost, the one she'd thought had fallen out of her dress.

She remembered now. She'd put it in the fold at her waist. She put her hand in that fold of her dress. And there it was! The special seashell.

"Take your time, Silvermist." Vidia tossed her hair. "It's not as if anyone's waiting."

"I was just thinking," Silvermist said in her old calm way. "And now, before I throw the ball, I have something to say."

The fairies and sparrow men gazed at her intently.

"I'm not sure if I had bad luck or just a few bad days. I'm not sure about these old superstitions at all. But there is one thing I do know. If you believe you'll have bad luck, then you'll have bad luck."

That was why it didn't make a difference if the curse was real or all in her mind.

Silvermist turned to leave the contest. She didn't care about winning or losing or proving anything to anybody.

"Poor, sweet Silvermist," Vidia said. "She can't go on. She's lost her nerve."

Well, thought Silvermist, *maybe I have to prove something to* one *fast-flying fairy.*

She turned her back to the target. Then she tossed the waterball over her shoulder. It soared through the air. Silvermist heard it hit and splash all over. All around her, fairies gasped in shock.

"Bull's-eye!" cried Fira.

Silvermist grinned. Had that been a lucky shot? She didn't know. And she didn't care.

Join Tinker Bell, Prilla
and all the other
Never Fairies in...

A Masterpiece
for Bess

Here is a fairy-sized preview
of the first chapter!

A

Masterpiece

for

Bess

"EVERYBODY! COME TO my room!"

Tinker Bell flew about the tearoom. In a silvery voice she called out to the fairies and sparrow men gathered around the tables.

Lily and Rosetta, two garden-talent fairies, looked up from their breakfast of elderberry scones.

"What's the hurry, Tink?" asked Lily.

"Bess has just painted my portrait –

and you've got to come and see it!"
Tinker Bell urged.

Rosetta and Lily looked at each other
in surprise. It wasn't every day that Bess
painted a new portrait! What was the
occasion? they wondered. But before they
could ask, Tink had darted out the
tearoom door and into the kitchen.

"Let's go," Rosetta said to Lily.
They followed Tink through the Home
Tree up to her room.

There the fairies packed themselves
in wing to wing, like honeybees in a hive.
They could see Bess, in her usual paint
splattered skirt, standing at the front of
the room. She was hanging a life-size,
five-inch painting of Tinker Bell.

"Isn't it amazing?" gushed Tink. She
flew up behind Lily and Rosetta and

landed with a bounce on her loaf-pan bed.

And indeed it was. Bess's painting was so lifelike, if a fairy hadn't known better, she might have thought there were *two* Tinks in the room. No detail – from the dimples in Tink's cheeks to her woven sweetgrass belt – was overlooked. What Tink loved most about the painting, though, were the gleaming metal objects piled all around her: pots, pans, kettles, and colanders. She felt as if she could almost pull each one out of the painting.

It was a perfect portrait, as everyone could see. Right away the oohs and aahs began to echo off the tin walls of Tink's room.

"It's lovely!" said Lily. "Bess, you've outdone yourself again!"

"You're too kind. Really," Bess said.

Her lemon yellow glow turned slightly tangerine as she blushed. As Pixie Hollow's busiest painter, she was used to praise. But she never tired of hearing it.

"It's just what Tink's room needed," added Gwinn, a decoration-talent fairy. She gazed around Tink's metal-filled room.

"What's the occasion?" asked Rosetta.

"Oh, no occasion, really," said Bess. She brushed her long brown bangs out of her violet eyes. "Tink fixed my best palette knife, and I wanted to do something nice in return."

All around her, the fairies murmured approvingly. Bess felt her heart swell with pride. *This is what art is all about*, she thought. Times like these made her work worthwhile.

"Personally, I don't see what the fuss

is for," a thorny voice said above the din. "Honestly, my little darlings, what's so great about a fairy standing still?"

Bess didn't have to turn around. She knew who the voice belonged to – and so did everybody else. Vidia, the fastest – and by far the meanest – of the fast-flying-talent fairies, came forward.

"Oh, Vidia," Tink said with a groan. "You wouldn't know fine art if it flew up and nipped you on the nose."

"Yeah, don't listen to her, Bess," Gwinn called out.

"It's OK," Bess assured them. "Every fairy is welcome to have her own opinion."

But as she looked at the portrait again, she frowned slightly. It wasn't that Vidia's criticism bothered her. She'd learned long ago to let the spiteful fairy's snide comments roll off her wings like dewdrops. But Vidia's remark had started the wheels in Bess's mind turning.

"You know…," Bess began.

She searched the room for Vidia. But the fairy had already flown away.

"'You know' what?" asked Tink.

Bess shook her head. She turned to Tink with a sunny grin. "There's a whole day ahead of us!" she said. "I don't know about you fairies, but I've got work to do."

Spreading her wings, she lifted into the air. "Thanks for coming, everyone," she called.

And with a happy wave, Bess zipped off to her studio.

Collect all the Disney Fairies books

Discover the story of the Never Fairies in Fairy Dust and the Quest for the Egg